The est Sleepover EVER!

Grosset & Dunlap

The
Best Sleepover
EVER!

Katharine Holabird
Helen Craig

Grosset & Dunlap

For Alexandra, Esther, Adam, and Jerry:
with tons of love and many happy memories—KH
To Norma Roe: a good friend to both me and Angelina—HC

GROSSET & DUNLAP
Published by the Penguin Group
Penguin Group (USA) Inc., 375 Hudson Street, New York, New York 10014, U.S.A.
Penguin Group (Canada), 90 Eglinton Avenue East, Suite 700, Toronto, Ontario, Canada M4P 2Y3
(a division of Pearson Penguin Canada Inc.)
Penguin Books Ltd, 80 Strand, London WC2R 0RL, England
Penguin Ireland, 25 St Stephen's Green, Dublin 2, Ireland
(a division of Penguin Books Ltd)
Penguin Group (Australia), 250 Camberwell Road, Camberwell, Victoria 3124, Australia
(a division of Pearson Australia Group Pty Ltd)
Penguin Books India Pvt Ltd, 11 Community Centre, Panchsheel Park, New Delhi - 110 017, Indi
Penguin Group (NZ), Cnr Airborne and Rosedale Roads, Albany, Auckland 1310, New Zealand
(a division of Pearson New Zealand Ltd)
Penguin Books (South Africa) (Pty) Ltd, 24 Sturdee Avenue, Rosebank, Johannesburg 2196, South Afi

Penguin Books Ltd, Registered Offices:
80 Strand, London WC2R 0RL, England

Library of Congress Control Number: 2005015570

ISBN 0-448-44016-4   10 9 8 7 6 5 4 3 2

Dear Diary,

I have a really-truly important secret to tell you, and that is—I'm going to have a sleepover—my very first! Nobody knows yet except my very best friend, Alice (because you can't keep secrets from your very best friend).

The problem is that my mom is still thinking about it (ugh).

She says I may not be grown-up enough yet (what?!).

Every day I beg her so sweetly, "Please, Mom!" and I definitely promise to do whatever she says and be an angel mouseling. I do hope hope hope she'll say yes!

A sleepover would be my dream come true.

But can you imagine this? Henry sneaked in while I was having my serious discussion with Mom! He has absolutely no manners whatsoever. Sometimes I wish I didn't have a little cousin.

"I JUST LOVE SLEEPOVERS!" Henry squeaked. "CAN I COME TOO?"

Horrors!

"There won't be any silly little boy mouselings at my sleepover," I told him.

Dear Diary,

Miss Lilly is planning something BIG at ballet school. I can feel it in my whiskers. She said we must all be ready to give a really-truly great performance soon. What could it be? Alice and I can't stop whispering about it at our ballet lessons.

Dear Diary,

All my Pretty Pleases worked! Today Mom said YES! I am so excited, I can't stop doing tailspins!!! Isn't that the best thing since cheddar cheese?

"You'll have to be responsible," Mom said.

"I'll be completely and definitely responsible!" I replied.

"We can't have the whole cottage turned upside down," she went on.

"I'll be the tidiest mouseling in all of Mouseland!" I promised.

"And everyone must be in bed by 10 p.m."

"I'll dance in my dreams," I agreed, hopping up and down.

"Does everybody like cheddarburgers and ice cream?" Mom asked.

"Yes, but can we have lots of scrumptious snacks too?" I added.

"Hmmm. I'll make my special healthy cake," said Mom. "Parsnip and turnip." Mom always likes me to eat especially healthy food.

"Could you add chocolate icing?" I asked.

Mom smiled. "That would be interesting," she agreed.

"You're the absolutely Best Mom Ever!" I said, and I gave her a huge hug.

Whoopee!

Dear Diary,

   Alice came over today and we scampered up to my room. I hung my "Definitely No Entry" sign on the door so we could meet in private. Some naughty little mouselings don't know what private means—my baby sister, Polly, for instance. Polly kept scrabbling to get into my room, so Alice had to tell her off.

   "This is a top-secret meeting!" Alice reminded her.

Then Polly absolutely howled until Mom said we had to look after her—which was totally not fair.

Since Alice and I are very responsible mouselings, we gave Polly some old crayons and stuff to play with. "If you don't make another SQUEAK you can have a jellymouse," I said.

My greedy little sister loves jellymice!

After that Polly was as good as gold and she didn't squeak even once while Alice and I scribbled down our stupendous ideas. Before we knew it we'd nearly gobbled up Alice's entire collection of jellymice. Yum!

Then naughty Polly burst into tears AGAIN because we forgot to give her anything—so I very kindly shared my last half a jellymouse with her. As Mom says, big sisters should always be a good example.

Angelina and Alice's Stupendous Sleepover Ideas:

* Face-painting—we'll be the most beautiful ballerinas ever!

* Dress up and dance in the garden

* Buy secret collection of yummy candy from Mrs. Thimble

* Midnight feast—with tons of PIZZA for energy!!!

* Don't forget Peanutty Passion ice cream— favorite treat

* Collect lots of pillows for pillow fights

* Read out loud: *Spookiest Storybook Ever*

Dear Diary,

Here's who's coming to my sleepover (Mom says three is definitely the limit):

Alice Nimbletoes—my very, very bestest
    Number 1 Best Friend
Flora Greyfur and Felicity Whiskers—Best
    Friends Numbers 2 and 3

I am NOT inviting my cousin Henry—because he's little and annoying and he's a boy! Polly is WAY too little and will be in bed soon after my friends arrive. And I am definitely NOT inviting Priscilla and Penelope Pinkpaws—they're too mean.

Alice and I made lovely invitations for Flora and Felicity and decorated them with stupendous stickers (candy, hearts, ribbons). And guess what? I made up my own poem!

Here's what my invitation says:

Please come to Angelina's sleepover
Date: Friday, May 2
Time: 6 p.m. – until Saturday noon

We'll dress up and dance
and do what we please!

We'll have ice cream and cake
and tons of nice cheese!

So remember the date—
we'll stay up very late!

Love, Angelina XXXOOO

It was easy-peasy! Alice and I skipped down the lane to the mailbox to mail the invitations, and I even blew a kiss to our crabby neighbor, Mrs. Hodgepodge—was she ever surprised!

Dear Diary,

I knew it, I absolutely knew it!

Miss Lilly told us her big secret today. "Darlinks," she said (Miss Lilly always calls us her darlinks), "I have something marvelous to tell you—my special ballet friend is coming to visit our little village. Do you know who that is?"

"Serena Silvertail!" shouted Alice. We all gasped.

"Yes, my darlinks." Miss Lilly smiled. "The brightest star of the Royal Ballet Company is coming here to Chipping Cheddar for a vacation. And we will entertain her with our own special production!"

We could hardly believe our furry ears! Serena Silvertail, the best and most beautiful ballerina in all of Mouseland, is really-truly coming to our ballet school!

Alice squeaked so loudly, I thought my ears would fall off. We all jumped up and down, we were so excited, and I accidentally stepped on Priscilla's tail.

"Ouch!" Priscilla howled. "Angelina hurt me!"

"Ooops, sorry!" I said. (Mom always says you should say sorry even when you don't feel like it—that shows you are grown-up and responsible.) All the other dancers stopped and stared. It was soooo embarrassing.

Miss Lilly examined Priscilla's tail for bruises and patted her on the head. I felt soooo jealous I even wished that I had a bruise on my tail too!

"Back to your positions, everyone," said Miss Lilly.

Priscilla stuck her tongue out at me and I stuck my tongue out back at her.

"Mouselings!" snapped Miss Lilly. "Let's see lovely paws and tails—now concentrate!"

"Yes, Angelina," snickered Priscilla.

"Yes, Angelina," snickered Penelope.

Aren't they just too too horrible?

Dear Diary,

Every day we practice until our paws are completely frazzled. Miss Lilly has decided we will perform *Snow White* for Serena Silvertail. I definitely LOVE ballet performances more than anything. The only problem is that Miss Lilly is holding those awful auditions. (That's when all the dancers try out for the best parts and HOPE HOPE HOPE Miss Lilly will choose them.)

14

I simply hate auditions! They are scary and make my tummy feel all rumbly and sick. Of course, Penelope and Priscilla Pinkpaws think that they're the very tip-top ballerinas, and they always show off for Miss Lilly and try to tease me.

They whisper stupid things like "Straighten your whiskers, Angelina!" and "Remember to smile, Angelina!" Can you imagine? Miss Lilly says ballerinas must always be disciplined, which means being tidy and on time and not screaming at the Pinkpaws or getting into fights—but how can you stop your tail twitching when you're upset?

Dear Diary,

It's a hard life being a ballerina sometimes—especially when there's so much else to think about (like sleepovers!).

Today I was starving after ballet lessons, so I had three pieces of cheddar-cheese pie when I came home.

Henry hopped into the kitchen with his silly Batmouse costume. (He's always at my house!) "I WANT SOME, TOO!" he squeaked, so Mom came rushing in with Polly.

Mom was in a bad mood and didn't even care about my hard day. "Please don't snack before supper, Angelina," she scolded.

"DON'T SNACK, ANGELINA," repeated Henry. What a copymouse he is! Grrrrr!

I made a face at him and he started howling, so Mom sent me up to my room. Imagine!

I threw myself on my bed and cried and

cried until Dad finally came home. We had a nice cuddle.

"Hmmm, I smell some yummy macaroni and cheese," Dad said.

Then I raced him downstairs, and I won! Dad and I absolutely LOVE macaroni and cheese—it's one of our tip-top favorites. (I'm secretly glad that Henry hates it.)

Dear Diary,

My sleepover is going to be next Friday—
I can hardly wait! Alice and Flora and
Felicity are definitely coming. We'll camp
out in my room and we can whisper and tell
secrets all night! Oh, and Alice and I are
thinking up crazy games—and we'll make our
own special pizzas for our midnight feast.

"My parents won't mind at all," I said.
"They'll be fast asleep."

Dear Diary,

Today Miss Lilly announced that auditions
for the *Snow White* ballet would be on
Saturday morning.

"Ooops," I whispered to Alice. "That's
the morning after my sleepover."

"I expect you all here at nine o'clock on
the dot," said Miss Lilly.

"What if someone's late?" asked
Priscilla, smiling in her usual icky way.

"Ballerinas have to be on time," said
Miss Lilly, "or they won't be able to dance."

"Uh-oh," I whispered to Alice.

"Oooh, Angelina's got a problem,"
snickered Penelope.

"No, I haven't!" I snapped.

"Doesn't that seem awfully early for
auditions?" asked Alice as we skipped home
after our ballet lesson.

"Yes," I agreed. "We'll need lots of alarm clocks."

"Good idea," said Alice. "Then we can stay up as late as we like."

"Definitely!" I agreed.

Dear Diary,

I can hardly believe I'm having a sleepover and dancing in *Snow White*. My life is just soooo exciting. Last night I couldn't sleep a wink. I watched the stars twinkling in the sky forever, but I still wasn't the least bit tired, so I danced around my room to calm myself down. Of course, I tried to be extra quiet, but somehow my toy shelf broke while I was practicing pirouettes. (Ooops!) It crashed to the floor and made a horrible racket.

Because I am a very responsible mouseling I picked up all the books and toys by myself. But then Dad came in, looking very very mad.

"Angelina, if you dance all night long I'll have to call Miss Lilly tomorrow and cancel ballet lessons," he said.

So I scampered into bed. My heart was absolutely aching. How unfair would that be?

Dear Diary,

Today was a great day—Mom and I went to Mrs. Thimble's shop and bought tons of cheddarburgers and Peanutty Passion ice cream and cheesy chips and really-truly yummy things to make pizza with. Of course, Mom also wants us to have healthy snacks like carrots and celery and raisins and nuts.

"Please can we buy lots of candy?" I begged.

"Don't worry, Angelina," Mom said. "There'll be plenty of parsnip-turnip cake."

(Ugh. I don't think Alice will like that idea very much—even if Mom puts chocolate icing on it.)

Mrs. Thimble was really impressed by all our shopping.

"I'm having my very first sleepover," I told Mrs. Thimble proudly.

"It looks as if you've invited the whole village," joked Mrs. Thimble.

She gave me a sugar mouse (scrumptious) and we all waved good-bye.

Dear Diary,

Today I went back to Mrs. Thimble's shop with Alice! Mrs. Thimble looked a bit surprised. Alice and I put all our saved-up pennies on the counter—and luckily we had enough for some very yummy goodies. Yippee! We bought all our tip-top favorites to share with Flora and Felicity.

It is definitely:

THE BEST CANDY COLLECTION EVER

- 8 cheddarmints
- 4 mousiepops
- 16 licorice whiskers
- 8 chocolate mouse-tails
- 12 squeaky sweets

(We were running out of pennies—but we still had enough for a few more . . .)

- 4 sugar mice
- 12 cherry berries

. . . and then we counted out our last pennies for four expensive blue-cheese fizzies.

Mrs. Thimble put all our candy in a plain brown bag.

"It's going to be the best sleepover ever!" we told her.

"I hope you won't have too many tummy aches," said Mrs. Thimble. (Ha ha ha—another joke!)

Then she gave us each a chewy cheesy-choc. I just love Mrs. Thimble!

Alice and I scampered home and hid the candy package under my bed. Stupendous.

Dear Diary,

I've been practicing soooo hard for the *Snow White* auditions, and I do my ballet exercises every single day. I will definitely LOVE being Snow White and dancing with the handsome prince at the front of the stage.

Today Miss Lilly said, "Good work, Angelina. I'm sure you'll be one of the stars of our production." (Secretly, I think Miss Lilly wants me to be Snow White too.) Yippee!

I was so happy, I did THREE completely perfect arabesques. Priscilla called me a show-off. What a nerve!

That Henry Mouseling is soooo annoying. He always comes to ballet lessons, and now Miss Lilly has decided he can come to the auditions too.

"Henry would be simply adorable in *Snow White*," said Miss Lilly with a sigh.

Can you imagine? Henry is the worst ballet dancer ever!

Dear Diary,

Today at ballet school Miss Lilly was in

such a strict mood.

"Everyone needs to have a good rest before the auditions on Saturday," she said.

Of course, Priscilla and Penelope smiled their ickiest smiles at her. "We'll be going to bed very early, Miss Lilly," they said ever so sweetly. (They are such fibbers!)

"And you, Angelina?" Miss Lilly asked. (Why did she pick on me?)

"Oh, I always get up very early," I said. Which is mostly true.

I wish I could tell Miss Lilly all about my sleepover . . . but she just wouldn't understand.

Flora, Felicity, and Alice were staring very hard at their ballet slippers.

"Good," said Miss Lilly. "I'll see you all here bright and early on Saturday morning."

Dear Diary,

Tonight's the night! I can hardly wait.

I was so responsible, I set the table and helped Mom make the parsnip-turnip cake. (It's not so bad really if you like parsnips or turnips—but I hate them!)

I reminded Mom that Polly needs to have an extra-early bedtime tonight.

"Be a good big sister and let Polly join your party for a little while," said Mom.

(Sometimes being a big sister is very difficult!)

P.S. the worst news is this—my cousin

Henry is trying to sneak into my sleepover. Mom says Aunt Lavender has an emergency and Henry is just coming to play. Play! I can't stand it! I cried buckets and buckets.

Mom said I had to learn that things don't always turn out the way I want them to. (That made me feel even worse.) Thank goodness Alice arrived. I told her the terrible news.

"Don't worry. Henry will fall asleep hours before we do," said Alice.

"He's definitely too young for a real grown-up sleepover," I agreed.

"I'm starving!" Alice said. "Where's all that food?" We decided we needed a little snack, so we had some cheesy chips, cheesy popcorn, cheese 'n' chocolate cookies, cheese puffs, and cheddar-cheese sandwiches. We even ate a few carrots and raisins! After that I felt a teeny bit better.

Alice and I blew up pink balloons (my favorite color) and decorated the whole cottage with pink and purple streamers. Dad came home and said it looked as if the circus was in town.

Dear Diary,

Well, my first ever sleepover party is really-truly over.

Do you want to know what happened?

When Flora and Felicity arrived we dressed up in pink tutus and painted our faces. We all leaped and pirouetted around the garden like beautiful ballerinas, but then Felicity wanted to be Snow White. She stomped off in a huff because Alice and Flora and I wanted to be Snow White too. Finally we decided there could be four Snow Whites.

I was the best ever big sister and let Polly be one of Snow White's little helpers.

Polly was so happy, she tried to do a twirl like me, but she crashed into Flora instead.

Of course, Polly had a complete tantrum and then Mrs. Hodgepodge shouted at us over the gate. "You naughty mouselings are disturbing the peace!" she complained.

After that Mom made us go inside.

The very worst moment of the whole night was when Aunt Lavender came over with Henry. They arrived just as Mom brought out all the yummiest food and everyone was about to eat. Of course, my little cousin Henry was very greedy and gobbled down more cheddarburgers than anyone else, and even ate up all the carrots and nuts and raisins.

Dad said, "That little Henry will grow up to be a real supermouse one day."

Sometimes I just HATE having a little cousin.

Then Mom proudly brought in her special surprise, parsnip-turnip cake. I was relieved to see it looked a lot better with chocolate icing.

"What's THAT?" whispered Alice as Mom gave everyone a big slice. Then Alice tried it and got a very weird look on her face. Mom went into the kitchen and Alice said

"Yuck!" and we all started giggling. "Hurry!" whispered Alice, and we stuffed our pieces of cake under the table.

"WHAT HAPPENED TO THE CAKE?" Henry squeaked.

"Shhh!" we shushed him. "It's a very big secret, Henry," I said. "And if you tell

anyone about it, we'll never show you where we hid our super candy collection."

Henry loves candy more than anything, so, of course, he promised to keep our secret.

After supper we raced one another upstairs and had a pillow fight. I accidentally whacked Flora a bit too hard and she burst into tears and sobbed, "I want to go home!"

Mom called Flora's mom and they had a long talk while Flora sat and sucked her thumb. Mom said Flora could go home, but then Flora wiped her nose and said, "I want to stay!"

While Mom was busy with Flora, naughty Polly crawled off by herself under the table, and guess what? She found our hidden parsnip-turnip cake and ate it all up!

Mom put Polly to bed and Polly was sick

sick sick. We all felt a bit sorry for her. (Thank goodness Mom didn't know about all the cake under the table.)

Mom and Dad suddenly got rather grumpy and said, "It's high time for all little mouselings to be quiet and get ready for bed."

Henry raced upstairs and Alice and I had to sit on him in case he was after our secret candy. He made such a ruckus, Dad decided to have a Serious Talk with me. (Grrrr, Henry!)

"No more squabbles, Angelina," Dad said— even though it really-truly wasn't my fault!

"Little ballerinas need to sleep now," he added. "You've got a big day tomorrow."

"Good night, Daddy!" I said in my sweetest little voice.

"I AM A BALLERINA TOO!" squeaked Henry, but nobody was paying attention.

Then we snuggled into our sleeping bags and made up scary stories about the lonely ghost of Chipping Cheddar. Flora hid under her pillow and said she would go home if we didn't stop. So I let her cuddle Mousie, my top favorite toy. We all practiced our ballet steps in front of the mirror. Henry wanted to be the prince in *Snow White*, so we sat on him again until he gave up.

"OKAY, I'LL BE A FRIENDLY DWARF!"
Henry squeaked.

"I'm hungry—it's time for our midnight
feast!" said Alice.

So we carefully tiptoed downstairs and
guess what? Mom and Dad were having a
nap on the sofa!

"Your father is a big snorer," said Alice.

"Shhh!" I warned her, but luckily he didn't wake up.

Then Alice had a great idea. "Let's mix up everything in the kitchen," she said.

So we made the first ever Cheesy-choc, Marshmallow, Popcorn, and Peanutty Passion Ice-Cream Pizza—it was very very messy, but soooo scrumptious!

The kitchen didn't exactly look tidy after our feast, but we were much too busy to clean up.

Henry scampered upstairs, searching for our hidden candy collection, and Alice and I had to keep catching him and sitting on him again. Then Felicity started a Bouncing Competition on my bed and we all bounced and bounced until something went BONG!

My bed sort of collapsed, but it was still good for bouncing, luckily.

Henry was by far the best at bouncing
and definitely didn't want to stop.

All of a sudden my whiskers started
drooping, and my tummy felt gruesome.

"Let's have our secret candy now!" Alice
whispered.

"HOORAY FOR CANDY!" squeaked Henry,
jumping up and down on my bed.

I had to curl up and hold my poor aching

tummy while Alice found our secret package under the collapsed bed and shared all my candy with Felicity and Flora.

Henry was very happy because he got to eat all of mine! Can you imagine?

When my tummy finally felt a teeny tiny bit better, my bedroom seemed very quiet.

The Best Candy Collection Ever was completely gobbled up, and three little mouselings were fast asleep on the floor. And there was my happy little cousin Henry, still dancing all by himself in front of my mirror!

"DO I LOOK LIKE THE PRINCE NOW?" Henry squeaked.

"Go to sleep!" I scolded him.

I had to search for a long time before I found Mousie all crumpled up under Flora. Then I checked my alarm clock (it was way past midnight!) and fell fast asleep with Mousie in my arms.

Dear Diary,

At the audition everyone watched in amazement as I danced and pirouetted completely perfectly.

Miss Lilly hugged me and said, "Angelina, you danced so beautifully that I've chosen YOU to be Snow White in our new production. Congratulations!"

All the other mouselings shouted, "Hooray for Angelina!" Even Priscilla and Penelope said they were happy I got the part.

Too bad that only happened in my dream—but it was the best dream ever!

What really happened was not like a beautiful dream at all . . .

I am sure sure sure that I set my alarm clock for eight o'clock in the morning, but I never heard a thing. In fact, we were all fast asleep, and I was dreaming about twirling across the stage in front of Serena Silvertail and Miss Lilly when I heard someone in my dream calling me—

"GET UP, ANGELINA!"

Henry was squeaking right into my ears!

I sat up in bed and rubbed my eyes. It was sunny outside, but Alice was snoring away and Flora and Felicity were still curled up, dreaming.

"IT'S TIME TO GO TO MISS LILLY'S!" Henry squeaked. "BYE!" Then he hopped downstairs and bounced out of the door.

I scrambled out of my bed and scampered madly around the room, tossing toys in the air and searching for my best pink tutu. When the others woke up, their eyes were red and their whiskers were rumpled. They definitely did NOT look like the best ballerinas in all of Mouseland.

"Where are my ballet slippers?"
cried Flora.

"I can't find my hair ribbons!"
moaned Felicity.

"What's for breakfast?" asked Alice
sleepily.

"Forget breakfast, Alice!" I snapped.
"The audition is starting!"

Alice leaped out of bed like a rocket.
She struggled into her tutu, threw on her
slippers, and flew out of the door and down
the stairs. (I never knew Alice could run so
fast.)

I raced after her, followed by Flora
and Felicity fussing about hair ribbons.

My mother was in her dressing gown
staring at the VERY BIG MESS we'd left in
the kitchen. Ooops. There was tons of food
everywhere, plus all sorts of dirty spoons
and forks and pots and pans and things.

Polly was happily exploring under the table again.

"See you soon, Mom!" I shouted as we scrambled past.

Thank goodness Miss Lilly's Ballet School is at No. 9 Chipping Cheddar Village Green in Chipping Cheddar Village—because that is very close to my cottage on Honeysuckle Lane. But it didn't seem close at all as we were racing to get to the audition.

When we finally arrived at Miss Lilly's Ballet School we were all panting and frazzled.

We were also very, very late.

Priscilla and Penelope were dancing gracefully across the stage when we straggled in.

"Shhh!" whispered Miss Lilly, pointing to some chairs at the back.

We all sat there fidgeting and worrying
horribly while Priscilla and Penelope danced
on and on.

Of course, the twins knew all the steps
to the *Snow White* ballet perfectly, and
everything from their glittery tutus to
their satin slippers was shiny and new.

I could see this was not my lucky day . . .

"Lovely dancing, Penelope and Priscilla,"
said Miss Lilly. "And next is . . . ?"

"ME!" Henry leaped on to the stage. He was still wearing his pajamas!

"All right, my darlink," said Miss Lilly. "Let's see what you can do."

Sometimes I have to admit my little cousin Henry is very brave. He really-truly doesn't understand that auditions are scary. Henry just danced all over that stage, showing off for Miss Lilly with a big smile on his face. For some reason Miss Lilly adores Henry. (All grown-ups adore my cousin Henry—which I simply cannot understand.)

Miss Lilly kept clapping her paws and cheering him on. "Can you do a little plié for us, Henry?" she asked.

Sure enough, Henry bent his little legs and put his paws over his head in a cute plié.

"Now show us an arabesque," Miss Lilly continued. And Henry did it!

In fact, Henry did everything almost perfectly, and I could see that Miss Lilly was totally amazed.

"Good work, Henry," said Miss Lilly.

"HOORAY!" shouted Henry.

Then Felicity started dancing, but she kept stumbling because her ribbons were undone.

I tried extra hard to concentrate. I sat very straight in my chair, pointed my toes, and squinted my eyes, but the stage looked fuzzy and I couldn't stop yawning. I shut my eyes for just a second and was about to have a very nice dream when Alice poked me in the ribs.

"It's your turn!" Alice whispered.

Every ear and whisker in the room turned toward me.

"Angelina," said Miss Lilly in a not-nice strict voice. "You were very late this morning, but I have decided to give you a chance to try out for the part."

"Thank you, Miss Lilly," I said.

I walked to the stage. My heart was

thumping and my tail dragged along the floor.

"You may begin," said Miss Lilly. "Music, please."

The piano sounded awfully loud, and the lights seemed much too bright. I peered out, looking for a friendly face, but Miss Lilly was not smiling at me the way she usually does, and the Pinkpaws twins were whispering together in a nasty way. I looked hopefully at Alice, but she was fast asleep in her chair— and so were Flora and Felicity.

Ballerinas always say, "The show must go on," which means you must try to do your very best, even if you feel completely horrid. Sadly, the show did not go on at the audition, because my dancing was totally gruesome. My legs felt like jelly and my tummy was all rumbly again. I tried to perk up my ears and smile, but I felt like crying the whole time. I managed to remember a few things properly— but only the very easiest ballet positions. I could hardly remember any of the special

Snow White dance steps I'd made up with my friends.

Even my usual stupendous leaps and twirls were too hard for me.

It was all like a very, very

horrible dream, and although I wanted
to be like Snow White dancing with the
prince, I was really-truly more like Sleeping
Beauty wishing she could lie down and sleep
for a hundred years.

And worst of all, I heard Henry
squeaking away in the front row, "COME
ON, ANGELINA—YOU CAN DO IT!" Can
you imagine?

At last it was over. I did my very best
curtsy for Miss Lilly, but sadly I tripped
getting off the stage and fell on Henry.

"Ooops, sorry!" I said, and gave him a
little hug.

"I'll let you know my decision next week
at ballet school," Miss Lilly told us. "After
you've all had a good sleep." Then she
thanked everyone for coming.

I was too ashamed to say anything
to her . . .

Dear Diary,

One thing about sleepovers that most mouselings don't understand is that there is really a lot of cleaning up to do after everyone goes home. Because Alice is my very best friend ever she agreed to help me. That was especially kind because we were both totally frazzled after the horrid audition.

Mom reminded me that a promise is a promise and gave us each a scrubbing brush and a bucket of soapy water. Then Alice and I swept and washed the kitchen and put away every single pot and pan.

"Maybe that midnight feast wasn't such a good idea," mumbled Alice as we emptied the garbage cans for the third time.

"Don't forget to sweep under the table," said Mom cheerfully.

"Ooops," I whispered to Alice. "How does she know?"

But I already thought I knew the answer.

Finally we finished and Alice straggled home, looking miserable. I went up to my room and crawled into my crooked, fallen-down bed. I was so tired, I didn't care that I didn't have a pillow and that my toys were all over the place. I couldn't see Mousie anywhere, and I was even too tired to start looking for her. I fell fast asleep upside down in my tutu, and I didn't have a single dream.

Dear Diary,

Today at ballet school Miss Lilly said, "Please sit down, mouselings, while I call your names."

I sat next to Alice and Flora, and their whiskers were trembling just like mine. We were so worried, we didn't even fidget the way we normally do.

Miss Lilly smiled and said she had a Big Announcement.

"Snow White will be danced by Priscilla," she said. (Oh, I felt unbelievably sad!)

"And the wicked queen will be Penelope," Miss Lilly continued.

How could Miss Lilly give the Pinkpaws twins the two very best parts? It's so unfair!

"At least Penelope gets to be really wicked," Alice whispered.

"Priscilla and Penelope danced very well at the audition, and they came on time!"

said Miss Lilly,
and she definitely
looked at me!

I stared at the
floor and tried
not to cry, but a
tear dripped off
my nose anyway.

My head was
buzzing horribly,
as if all sorts of nasty bees were zooming
around my brain, and I could hardly hear
Miss Lilly speaking.

"Angelina," said Miss Lilly, "you seemed
to have a few problems this time."

"I know, Miss Lilly," I answered, choking
back more horrid tears.

"But you are a very good dancer," Miss
Lilly continued, "and I want you to be the
leader of Snow White's friendly dwarfs."

I couldn't believe my furry ears!

"Excuse me, Miss Lilly," I said, "but—"

"No buts, Angelina," said Miss Lilly. "You will be Sleepy, and Alice Nimbletoes will be Grumpy."

I didn't hear the rest of Miss Lilly's list. Alice and I stared at each other.

We knew that Miss Lilly wouldn't tell us a bad joke, or fib.

"I'M SO HAPPY, ANGELINA!"

I looked up, and there was Henry jumping up and down.

"Why?" I asked.

"I GOT THE PART!" he squeaked. "I'M DOPEY AND YOU'RE SLEEPY AND ALICE—"

"I know, Henry," I said.

"SO WE CAN ALL DANCE TOGETHER!" Henry squeaked on.

"Yes," I said, really trying to be brave, "I guess we can."

Dear Diary,

Today Mom said I could make a bouquet for Miss Lilly, and I picked the prettiest daisies in our garden. Then I went and knocked on the door of Miss Lilly's cottage. Even though it's not much fun to say, "I've

been really-truly stupid," I would do
anything for Miss Lilly.

"Thank you, Angelina, darlink," said Miss
Lilly. "These are lovely flowers."

"I'm so sorry," I said, trying to smile. "I
made a terrible mistake."

"Come inside, Angelina," said Miss Lilly.
"We need to talk."

Then I told Miss Lilly all about my sleepover and how exciting it was and how we stayed up too late.

"But we still tried our best at the audition," I said.

"I know you did," said Miss Lilly, and she gave me a hug. "And I think you've learned an important lesson."

"I guess dancers do need some sleep," I said, "if they really-truly want to dance."

Dear Diary,

We are soooo busy at rehearsals that I have sore paws from so much ballet dancing. It's hard to be just one of seven dwarfs instead of the beautiful Snow White. At least I get to be with my friends, because we are all dwarfs.

Henry is good at being Dopey. He wiggles his tail and hops all over the stage. And even though Henry is a silly little boy mouseling, he can be kind sometimes. He smiles and squeaks at me, "YOU'RE A GREAT DANCER, ANGELINA!" whenever I feel terribly sad about being the leader of the dwarfs.

Anyway, Alice likes being Grumpy because we're always together and we can whisper during rehearsals. She doesn't mind wearing a beard and baggy pants—it makes her giggle. Felicity and Flora are not too thrilled to be dancing dwarfs, though, especially as our costumes are not exactly beautiful. We definitely don't look pretty in this ballet!

Of course, Priscilla looks exactly like a princess in her glittery Snow White costume. And she is soooo stuck-up about it! She hardly speaks to anyone now that she's Snow White. She just sniffs and prances past as if we are all invisible—even though we are supposed to be the ones who have saved her!

Penelope enjoys giving everyone nasty looks, and she's very happy when Priscilla eats the poisoned apple and falls over.

Dear Diary,

Serena Silvertail is coming to Chipping Cheddar tomorrow!

I'm afraid she will think I'm not a good dancer because I have such a small part in the show. This morning Mom said she can still remember being miserable when she didn't win first prize for singing at her school. (Imagine!) Mom said she's proud of me for dancing my best as Sleepy, even though I am soooo disappointed not to be Snow White.

Dear Diary,

Today Miss Lilly's Ballet School in Chipping Cheddar, Mouseland, performed *Snow White and the Seven Dwarfs* for the prima ballerina of Mouseland, Miss Serena Silvertail.

Serena Silvertail is just like a princess. She smiled the most beautiful sparkly smile at everyone, even the littlest mouselings, and she watched our performance as if it were the most exciting thing she'd ever seen.

Miss Lilly was so nervous, she madly raced around backstage like the rest of us, and she almost forgot her speech. But when the curtain opened, Miss Lilly took a deep breath and remembered every word—I was very proud of her.

Even though I couldn't be Snow White I put my whole heart into the performance. That is what Miss Lilly calls being professional. In fact, all of the seven dwarfs were definitely professional. We enjoyed being the funny dancers and making the audience laugh, and we got lots of cheers at the end.

Priscilla and Penelope were not too bad either, even though they have such icky smiles. Just before the show, the twins got into a big argument backstage about who was the prettiest one. Priscilla got so upset that she stomped on stage looking really mad, so I think Miss Lilly will have a Serious Talk with them later!

Of course, my parents came even though I told them not to bother. They said it couldn't have been so easy to dance with a beard on.

The best part was after the performance, when Serena Silvertail came backstage.

"You all did so well," she said with her sparkly smile. "Every single one of you. Miss Lilly is a wonderful teacher—but you each have to do the hard work yourself."

We all curtsied and shook Serena Silvertail's lovely paws (she has so many rings!) and then it was time to change and go home.

"Angelina," Miss Lilly called me from the dressing room. "Someone wants to speak with you."

Then something absolutely amazing happened. I was invited to the Pink Peppermint Tea Parlor by Serena Silvertail!

Imagine!

"Miss Lilly told me about your sleepover and the audition, Angelina," said Serena Silvertail as we sat down, while Miss Lilly ordered tea and crumpets.

"Oh dear," I said. I felt soooo embarrassed.

"The funny thing is," Serena Silvertail continued, "I made the very same mistake when I was a mouseling!"

I could not believe my furry ears. Would Serena Silvertail tell me such a big fib?

"Really?" I asked, my eyes popping out of my head.

"Definitely," she said, sipping her blackberry tea. "The night before the *Cindermouse* audition I stayed up very late with my friends. We had the best sleepover ever!"

"Did you get the part?" I asked.

"Of course not," said Serena Silvertail. "I could hardly keep my eyes open the next morning, and I couldn't dance at all. I got the part of the coachmouse and Fenella Furball was chosen as Cindermouse. I was so ashamed of myself!"

I looked at Miss Lilly and she nodded,

so I knew it was true.

Suddenly I felt like the luckiest mouseling in all of Mouseland. It was hard to believe that it was really-truly me, Angelina, drinking blackberry tea in china cups and nibbling buttery crumpets and strawberry jam with Miss Lilly and Serena Silvertail at the Pink Peppermint Tea Parlor.

I found out that Serena Silvertail is not only the most wonderful ballet dancer, but she has a very kind heart as well. Everything she said made me feel better and better and better until all my horrid feelings just seemed to fly away.

"Don't be afraid to make mistakes," Serena Silvertail told me. "Whatever happens, just keep trying." And then she patted me on the head.

When at last it was time to leave the Pink Peppermint Tea Parlor, I was so happy, I just skipped out of the door with Miss Lilly and Serena Silvertail.

The Pinkpaws twins were passing by with their mother. They all stopped and stared—which was rather rude. But I smiled and waved at them anyway.

"Thank you, Miss Lilly," I said, giving my

ballet teacher a hug.

"And thank you too, Serena Silvertail," I continued, doing my very best curtsy.

"It was a pleasure," said Serena Silvertail with her sparkly smile. "And remember, the most important thing is to keep on dancing!"

"I will!" I said.

Then I twirled off down the street . . . because I definitely had lots of dancing to do.

Look out for the next truly stupendous
Angelina's Diary *adventure—coming soon!*

Angelina's Diary

A Party for the Princess

Dear Diary,

Can you imagine what it's like to be a
real-true princess?

The Queen of Mouseland is throwing the biggest
party ever at the palace, for Princess Sophie's
birthday—and Angelina has been invited!

But Angelina isn't having that much fun—the
food is yucky, Priscilla Pinkpaws is being mean, and
Angelina is missing her bestest friend, Alice.

Angelina is determined to find a friend
somewhere in the palace. Who will it be?